never
take a
BEAR
to school

For Jago
M.S.

For Vincent
B.T.

ORCHARD BOOKS

First published in Great Britain in 2017 by The Watts Publishing Group

1 3 5 7 9 10 8 6 4 2

Text © Mark Sperring, 2017
Illustrations © Britta Teckentrup, 2017

The moral rights of the author and illustrator have been asserted.

A CIP catalogue record for this book is available from the British Library.

ISBN HB 978 1 40833 972 5 PB 978 1 40833 973 2

Printed and bound in China

Orchard Books
An imprint of Hachette Children's Group
Part of The Watts Publishing Group Limited
Carmelite House, 50 Victoria Embankment, London EC4Y 0DZ

An Hachette UK Company
www.hachette.co.uk

never
take a
BEAR
to school

MARK SPERRING   **BRITTA TECKENTRUP**

ORCHARD

On your **very first day** there is one simple rule,

You just cannot take your bear into school.

It might seem unfair and slightly unkind

But there are very **good reasons** to leave him behind.

Imagine the scene, what panic he'll cause,
When he runs through the playground, waving his paws!

He can't sit at a desk, however he tries.

The chairs are **too little,** just girl and boy sized!

He won't stop to listen, when he's asked to **hush**.

He'll **growl** and he'll **grizzle** and cause such a fuss!

At lunchtime, he'll eat every last scrap of food,
Leaving **nothing** for **anyone**...

how VERY rude!

In gym class his jumping

will give tots a scare.

No one wants tootsies

squashed flat by a bear!

So, please, please believe me,

although it sounds fun,

Bears can't go to school.

No, it just isn't done!

But try not to fret as your first day begins,

For soon you'll be busy with all sorts of things . . .

Like greeting your teacher,

then taking your seat,

And saying **hello** to the new friends you'll meet.

Like painting a picture of what you love best,

And hanging it proudly along with the rest.

Like hearing a story,

and doing your sums.

Who would have thought school could be
so much fun!

Then the bell **rings** and your first school day ends.

It's time to say **goodbye** to all your new friends . . .

You run to the school gates.

Look, who's waiting there?

With a **BIG HAIRY HUG** . . .

Yes! Yes! It's your bear!

You walk home describing your very first day,

Amazing, surprising, in so many ways.

And though you have missed him,
just like he's missed you,

You've made **lots of friends** and **learnt something too.**

And now you're back home,
all **cosy together,**

Each moment you share

is more **precious** than ever.

It's lovely to know that he'll always be there,

Whenever you need him,

because he's

YOUR BEAR!